I'm Your Flag, So Please Treat Me Right!

published by

NATIONAL CENTER for
YOUTH ISSUES

www.ncyi.org

To my dad, Lou Lorenz, WWII Veteran, U.S. Navy – Julia

Folding the US Flag for storage

1. Begin by holding the flag waist-high with another person, so that its surface is parallel to the ground.

2. Fold the lower half of the stripe section lengthwise over the field of stars, holding the bottom and top edges securely.

3. Fold the flag again lengthwise with the blue field on the outside.

4. Make a rectangular fold, then a triangular fold, by bringing the striped corner of the folded edge to meet the open top edge of the flag, starting the fold from the left side.

5. Turn the outer end point inward, parallel to the open edge, to form a second triangle.

6. The triangular folding is continued until the entire length of the flag is folded in this manner (usually thirteen triangular folds). On the final fold, any remnant that does not neatly fold into a triangle (or in the case of exactly even folds), the last triangle is tucked into the previous fold.

7. When the flag is completely folded, only a triangular blue field of stars should be visible.

NATIONAL CENTER for YOUTH ISSUES

P.O. Box 22185
Chattanooga, TN 37422-2185
423.899.5714 • 866.318.6294
fax: 423.899.4547 • www.ncyi.org

ISBN: 978-1-937870-29-4 $9.95
© 2014 National Center for Youth Issues, Chattanooga, TN
All rights reserved.
Written by: Julia Cook
Illustrations by: Michelle Hazelwood Hyde
Design by: Phillip W. Rodgers
Contributing Editor: Beth Spencer Rabon • Jennifer Deshler
Contributing Illustrator: Kay Tyson Caldwell
Published by National Center for Youth Issues • Softcover
Printed at Starkey Printing, Chattanooga, Tennessee, U.S.A., June 201

I am a flag…but not just any flag…I am AMERICA's flag! The United States of America, that is!

I'm the symbol for who we are as a people. I stand for Life, Liberty, and the Pursuit of Happiness! My bright stars and powerful stripes connect all of us as Americans.

I stand for freedom when I wave in the air, so proud of my stars and stripes.
Whenever you see me, please show that you care.

I'm your flag, so please treat me right!

The White House

Washington Monument

U.S. Capitol

I'm lucky to have you and you're lucky to have me.
The things that I stand for are why you are free.

Jefferson Memorial

Arlington National Cemetery
The Tomb of the Unknowns

HERE RESTS IN
HONORED GLORY
AN AMERICAN
SOLDIER

Be proud when you see my
red, *white,* and **blue**.

When I wave in the air…I'm waving for YOU!

I didn't always look like this.
When I was younger, I looked different.

I've always had 13 red and white stripes…one for each of the 13 colonies that declared their independence from Great Britain. My **red** stripes stand for **hardiness** and **valor**. That means I am tough and brave. My white stripes stand for purity and innocence. That means that I am dirt free, full of goodness, and I will do no harm.

Back in 1776, when Betsy Ross
first made me, I only had 13 stars.

As I grew up, I kept changing. Now my blue part is decorated with 50 stars...one for every state! My blue part is called my **UNION**. My **blue** color stands for **vigilance**, **perseverance**, and **justice**.

That's because I am watchful and alert, I never give up, and I want everyone to be treated with fairness.

I stand for freedom when I wave in the air,
so proud of my stars and stripes.

Whenever you see me,
please show that you care.

I'm your flag, so please treat me right!

I'm lucky to have you and you're lucky to have me
The things that I stand for are why you are free.

Be proud when you see my red, **white**, and *blue*.
When I wave in the air...I'm waving for YOU!

Iwo Jima

Neil Armstrong: First Man on the Moon

Washington Crossing
the Delaware

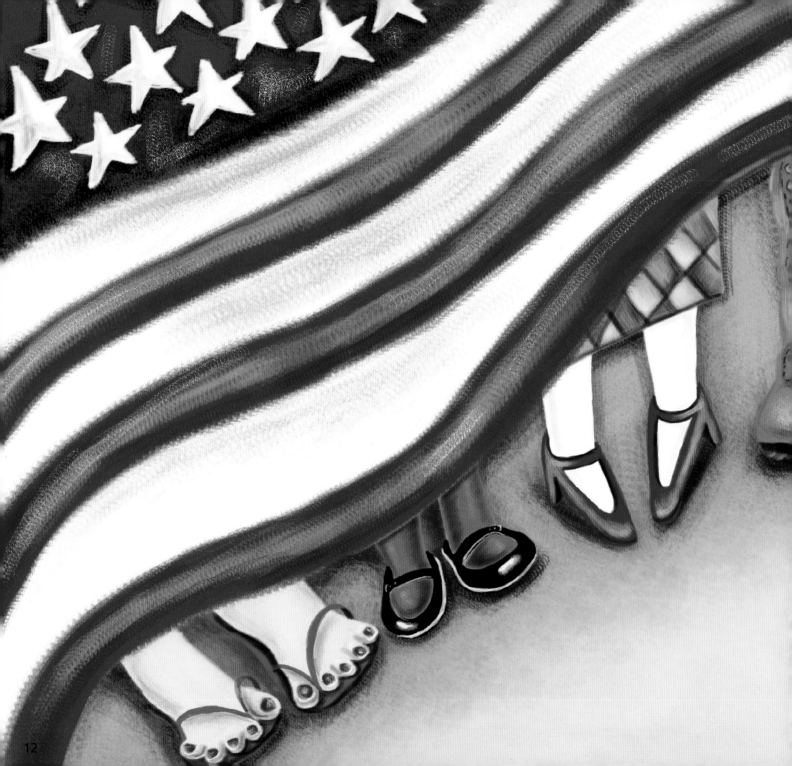

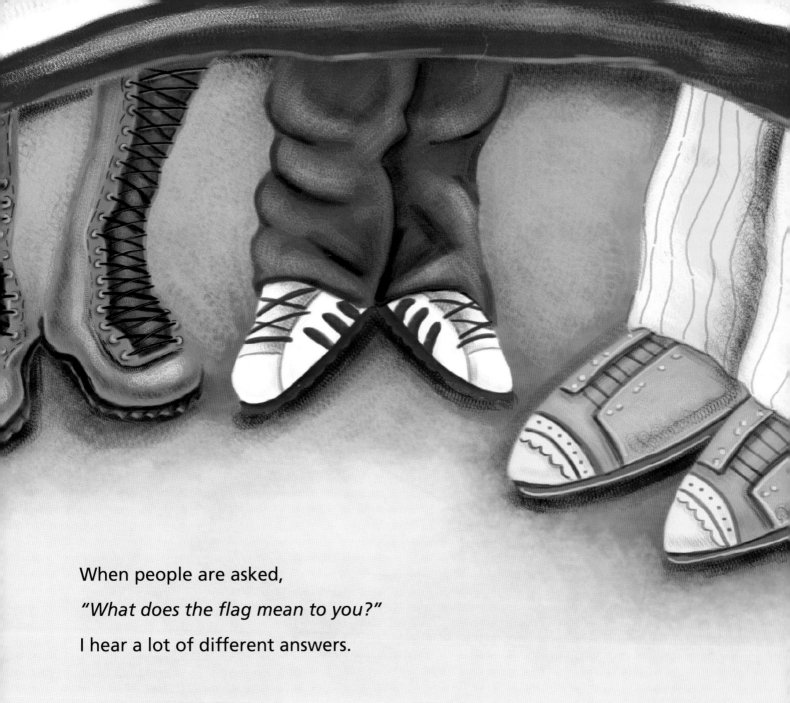

When people are asked,

"What does the flag mean to you?"

I hear a lot of different answers.

"When I see the flag, it makes me feel proud!

I love my country and I want to shout it out loud!"

*"When I see the flag,
I feel safe inside.*

*It protects me from harm
and serves as my guide."*

"To me, the flag screams

I AM FREE!

Free to become all that I want to be!"

Ground Zero 9/11

"When I see the flag, it reminds me of hope.

It gives me the strength that I need to cope."

"To me, the flag means love and acceptance for **some**.

Until it's for **ALL**, our work is not done (and we still have a ways to go!)"

17

Every person has their own unique idea of what I mean to them and that's the way it's supposed to be! I am the symbol for who we are as a people, and my bright stripes and powerful stars connect all of us as **Americans!**

*I stand for freedom when I wave in the air,
so proud of my stars and stripes.*

*Whenever you see me,
please show that you care.*

I'm your flag, so please treat me right!

The best way to treat me right is to show that you have respect for me.

Never let me touch the ground.

Replace me when I'm all worn out.

Whenever you choose to fly me at night, don't forget to shine me with light.

It's not that I'm afraid of the dark.
It's not right to hide my stripes and my stars.

19

Never use me to make your clothes.

But you can paint pictures of me on your toes.

20

Never pin me up on a ceiling.
The sky is my limit and that causes hurt feelings.

Be energetic when you raise me up on my pole.
Lower me down slowly 'cause you're sad when I go.

21

When you fly me at half-mast
as a sign of respect,

Pull me up all the way first
and show no regrets.

Then lower me down slowly,
to just the right spot.

When I fly at half-mast,
it comes with great thought.

Whenever you lower me down off my pole,
I need to be treated special, you know.

You must fold me up in just the right way,
So I'm ready to fly for you the next day.

There are instructions on how to fold me
in the front of this book. Just read them
and then you'll know what to do!

On Columbus Day in 1892, all of the schools in America started saying the Pledge of Allegiance to the flag.

That's Me.

When you say the Pledge, you're making a promise (*PLEDGE*) to be loyal (*ALLEGIANCE*) to our country, and you're recognizing how lucky we are to be able to choose our own leaders (*REPUBLIC*). You're also recognizing that we as Americans stick together (*INDIVISIBLE*), and that because others have sacrificed so much, we are now treated with fairness (*JUSTICE*).

When you stand up tall, place your right hand over your heart and look at me when you are saying the Pledge of Allegiance; it shows that you really do mean what you are saying.

I'm lucky to have you and you're lucky to have me.

The things that I stand for are why you are free.

Be proud when you see my **red**, *white*, and **blue**.

When I wave in the air...**I'm waving for YOU!**

So many sacrifices have had to be made,
so that I can be here for you on this day.

I'm worth a lot, so keep doing your part,
and always keep me close to your heart.

I stand for freedom when I wave in the air,
so proud of my stars and stripes.

Whenever you see me,
please show that you care.

I'm your flag, so please
treat me right!

In CONGRESS, July 4, 1776.

A DECLARATION

By the REPRESENTATIVES of the

UNITED STATES OF AMERICA,

In GENERAL CONGRESS ASSEMBLED.

"We hold these truths to be self-evident, that all men are created equal, that they are endowed by their Creator with certain unalienable Rights, that among these are Life, Liberty and the pursuit of Happiness."

THE PATRIOT FOUNDATION TRUST

EXTENDING LIBERTY TO THE NEXT GENERATION

"Our cause is noble; it is the cause of mankind!" (George Washington, 1779)

"Liberty must at all hazards be supported.
We have a right to it, derived from our Maker.
But if we had not, our fathers have earned and bought it for us,
at the expense of their ease, their estates, their pleasure, and their blood."

John Adams, 1765

Patriot Foundation Trust is pleased to sponsor "I'm Your Flag, So Please Treat Me Right," an outstanding educational resource for teaching young people a bit of our noble flag's history as our national banner, and how to honor it accordingly.

Our educational mission is to affirm individual Liberty, advocate for restoration of constitutional limits on government and the judiciary, and promote free enterprise, national defense, and traditional American values. Our objective is to restore the First Principles of Liberty, the endowed Rights of all People affirmed in our Declaration of Independence, enshrined in our Constitution, and secured by solemn oath "to support and defend" by generations of American Patriots since the formation of our nation.

More than a million American Patriots have given their lives to secure our freedom under the American flag.

In support of our mission, we produce two highly acclaimed pocket guides for students of all ages. The first, "The Patriot's Primer on Liberty," contains an inspiring introduction to Liberty by Mark Alexander, the text of our nation's founding documents, and many other resources. The second, "Founders' Wisdom," is a supplement with key historic quotes, speeches, and proclamations affirming Liberty.

Both guides are indispensable pocket references and educational tools for promoting the integrity of our Constitution and the Rule of Law it established.

For more information on receiving bulk orders of "The Patriot's Primer on Liberty" and "Founders' Wisdom," visit: PatriotFoundationTrust.org

Help us extend Liberty to the next generation!